D1146938

"'God has given me
blood to drink," she
said to the nurse,
and the nurse said,
"Don't rinse your
mouth or it won't clot"'

SHIRLEY JACKSON
Born 14 December 1916, San Francisco, California
Died 8 August 1965, Bennington, Vermont

All stories first published in *The Lottery and Other Stories*, 1949.

ALSO PUBLISHED BY PENGUIN BOOKS
The Haunting of Hill House · *We Have Always Lived in the Castle*

SHIRLEY JACKSON

The Tooth

PENGUIN BOOKS

PENGUIN CLASSICS

Published by the Penguin Group
Penguin Books Ltd, 80 Strand, London WC2R ORL, England
Penguin Group (USA) Inc., 375 Hudson Street, New York, New York 10014, USA
Penguin Group (Canada), 90 Eglinton Avenue East, Suite 700, Toronto, Ontario,
Canada M4P 2Y3 (a division of Pearson Penguin Canada Inc.)
Penguin Ireland, 25 St Stephen's Green, Dublin 2, Ireland
(a division of Penguin Books Ltd)
Penguin Group (Australia), 250 Camberwell Road, Camberwell, Victoria 3124, Australia
(a division of Pearson Australia Group Pty Ltd)
Penguin Books India Pvt Ltd, 11 Community Centre, Panchsheel Park,
New Delhi – 110 017, India
Penguin Group (NZ), 67 Apollo Drive, Rosedale, North Shore 0632, New Zealand (a
division of Pearson New Zealand Ltd)
Penguin Books (South Africa) (Pty) Ltd, 24 Sturdee Avenue, Rosebank, Johannesburg
2196, South Africa

Penguin Books Ltd, Registered Offices: 80 Strand, London WC2R ORL, England

www.penguin.com

Selected from *The Lottery and Other Stories*, first published in
Penguin Classics 2009
This edition published in Penguin Classics 2011
3

Typeset by Jouve (UK), Milton Keynes
Printed in England by Clays Ltd, St Ives plc

ISBN: 978-0-141-19599-5

www.greenpenguin.co.uk

Penguin Books is committed to a sustainable future
for our business, our readers and our planet.
The book in your hands is made from paper
certified by the Forest Stewardship Council.

Contents

The Tooth   1

The Witch   31

Charles   39

The Lottery   47

The Intoxicated   63

The Tooth

The bus was waiting, panting heavily at the curb in front of the small bus station, its great blue-and-silver bulk glittering in the moonlight. There were only a few people interested in the bus, and at that time of night no one passing on the sidewalk: the one movie theatre in town had finished its show and closed its doors an hour before, and all the movie patrons had been to the drugstore for ice cream and gone on home; now the drugstore was closed and dark, another silent doorway in the long midnight street. The only town lights were the street lights, the lights in the all-night lunchstand across the street, and the one remaining counter lamp in the bus station where the girl sat in the ticket office with her hat and coat on, only waiting for the New York bus to leave before she went home to bed.

Standing on the sidewalk next to the open door of the bus, Clara Spencer held her husband's arm nervously. 'I feel so funny,' she said.

'Are you all right?' he asked. 'Do you think I ought to go with you?'

'No, of course not,' she said. 'I'll be all right.' It was hard for her to talk because of her swollen jaw; she kept a handkerchief pressed to her face and held hard to her husband. 'Are you sure *you*'ll be all right?' she asked. 'I'll be back tomorrow night at the latest. Or else I'll call.'

'Everything will be fine,' he said heartily. 'By tomorrow noon it'll all be gone. Tell the dentist if there's anything wrong I can come right down.'

'I feel so funny,' she said. 'Light-headed, and sort of dizzy.'

'That's because of the dope,' he said. 'All that codeine, and the whisky, and nothing to eat all day.'

She giggled nervously. 'I couldn't comb my hair, my hand shook so. I'm glad it's dark.'

'Try to sleep in the bus,' he said. 'Did you take a sleeping pill?'

'Yes,' she said. They were waiting for the bus driver to finish his cup of coffee in the lunchstand; they could see him through the glass window, sitting at the counter, taking his time. 'I feel so *funny*,' she said.

'You know, Clara,' he made his voice very weighty, as though if he spoke more seriously his words would carry more conviction and be therefore more comforting, 'you know, I'm glad you're going down to New

York to have Zimmerman take care of this. I'd never forgive myself if it turned out to be something serious and I let you go to this butcher up here.'

'It's just a *toothache*,' Clara said uneasily, 'nothing very serious about a *toothache*.'

'You can't tell,' he said. 'It might be abscessed or something; I'm sure he'll have to pull it.'

'Don't even talk like that,' she said, and shivered.

'Well, it looks pretty bad,' he said soberly, as before. 'Your face so swollen, and all. Don't you worry.'

'I'm not worrying,' she said. 'I just feel as if I were all tooth. Nothing else.'

The bus driver got up from the stool and walked over to pay his check. Clara moved toward the bus, and her husband said, 'Take your time, you've got plenty of time.'

'I just feel funny,' Clara said.

'Listen,' her husband said, 'that tooth's been bothering you off and on for years; at least six or seven times since I've known you you've had trouble with that tooth. It's about time something was done. You had a toothache on our honeymoon,' he finished accusingly.

'Did I?' Clara said. 'You know,' she went on, and laughed, 'I was in such a hurry I didn't dress properly. I have on old stockings and I just dumped everything into my good pocketbook.'

3

'Are you sure you have enough money?' he said.

'Almost twenty-five dollars,' Clara said. 'I'll be home tomorrow.'

'Wire if you need more,' he said. The bus driver appeared in the doorway of the lunchroom. 'Don't worry,' he said.

'Listen,' Clara said suddenly, 'are you *sure* you'll be all right? Mrs Lang will be over in the morning in time to make breakfast, and Johnny doesn't need to go to school if things are too mixed up.'

'I know,' he said.

'Mrs Lang,' she said, checking on her fingers. 'I called Mrs Lang, I left the grocery order on the kitchen table, you can have the cold tongue for lunch and in case I don't get back Mrs Lang will give you dinner. The cleaner ought to come about four o'clock, I won't be back so give him your brown suit and it doesn't matter if you forget but be sure to empty the pockets.'

'Wire if you need more money,' he said. 'Or call. I'll stay home tomorrow so you can call at home.'

'Mrs Lang will take care of the baby,' she said.

'Or you can wire,' he said.

The bus driver came across the street and stood by the entrance to the bus.

'Okay?' the bus driver said.

'Good-bye,' Clara said to her husband.

'You'll feel all right tomorrow,' her husband said. 'It's only a toothache.'

'I'm fine,' Clara said. 'Don't you worry.' She got on the bus and then stopped, with the bus driver waiting behind her. 'Milkman,' she said to her husband. 'Leave a note telling him we want eggs.'

'I will,' her husband said. 'Good-bye.'

'Good-bye,' Clara said. She moved on into the bus and behind her the driver swung into his seat. The bus was nearly empty and she went far back and sat down at the window outside which her husband waited. 'Good-bye,' she said to him through the glass, 'take care of yourself.'

'Good-bye,' he said, waving violently.

The bus stirred, groaned, and pulled itself forward. Clara turned her head to wave good-bye once more and then lay back against the heavy soft seat. Good Lord, she thought, what a thing to do! Outside, the familiar street slipped past, strange and dark and seen, unexpectedly, from the unique station of a person leaving town, going away on a bus. It isn't as though it's the first time I've ever been to New York, Clara thought indignantly, it's the whisky and the codeine and the sleeping pill and the toothache. She checked hastily to see if her codeine tablets were in her pocketbook; they had been standing, along with the aspirin and a glass of water, on the dining-room sideboard, but somewhere in the lunatic flight from her home she must have picked them up, because they were in her pocketbook now, along with the twenty-odd dollars and her compact and comb and lipstick. She could tell from the feel of the lipstick that she had brought the old, nearly finished one, not the new one that was a darker shade and had cost two-fifty. There was a run in her stocking and a hole in the toe that she never noticed at home wearing her old comfortable shoes, but which was now suddenly and disagreeably apparent inside her best walking shoes. Well, she thought, I can buy new stockings in New York tomorrow, after the tooth is fixed, after everything's all right. She put her tongue cautiously on the tooth and was rewarded with a split-second crash of pain.

The bus stopped at a red light and the driver got out of his seat and came back toward her. 'Forgot to get your ticket before,' he said.

'I guess I was a little rushed at the last minute,' she said. She found the ticket in her coat pocket and gave it to him. 'When do we get to New York?' she asked.

'Five-fifteen,' he said. 'Plenty of time for breakfast. One-way ticket?'

'I'm coming back by train,' she said, without seeing why she had to tell him, except that it was late at night and people isolated together in some strange prison like a bus had to be more friendly and communicative than at other times.

'Me, I'm coming back by bus,' he said, and they both laughed, she painfully because of her swollen face. When he went back to his seat far away at the front of the bus she lay back peacefully against the seat. She could feel the sleeping pill pulling at her; the throb of the toothache was distant now, and mingled with the movement of the bus, a steady beat like her heartbeat which she could hear louder and louder, going on through the night. She put her head back and her feet up, discreetly covered with her skirt, and fell asleep without saying good-bye to the town.

She opened her eyes once and they were moving almost silently through the darkness. Her tooth was pulsing steadily and she turned her cheek against the cool back of the seat in weary resignation. There was a thin line of lights along the ceiling of the bus and no other light. Far ahead of her in the bus she could see the other people sitting; the driver, so far away as to be only a tiny figure at the end of a telescope, was straight at the wheel, seemingly awake. She fell back into her fantastic sleep.

She woke up later because the bus had stopped, the end of that silent motion through the darkness so positive a shock that it woke her stunned, and it was a minute before the ache began again. People were moving along the aisle of the bus and the driver, turning around, said, 'Fifteen minutes.' She got up and followed everyone else out, all but her eyes still asleep, her feet moving without awareness. They were stopped beside an all-night restaurant, lonely and lighted on the vacant road. Inside, it was warm and busy and full of people. She saw a seat at the end of the counter and sat down, not aware that she had fallen asleep again when someone sat down next to her and touched her arm. When she looked around foggily he said, 'Traveling far?'

'Yes,' she said.

He was wearing a blue suit and he looked tall; she could not focus her eyes to see any more.

'You want coffee?' he asked.

She nodded and he pointed to the counter in front of her where a cup of coffee sat steaming.

'Drink it quickly,' he said.

She sipped at it delicately; she may have put her face down and tasted it without lifting the cup. The strange man was talking.

'Even farther than Samarkand,' he was saying, 'and the waves ringing on the shore like bells.'

'Okay, folks,' the bus driver said, and she gulped quickly at the coffee, drank enough to get her back into the bus.

When she sat down in her seat again the strange man sat down beside her. It was so dark in the bus that the lights from the restaurant were unbearably glaring and she closed her eyes. When her eyes were shut, before she fell asleep, she was closed in alone with the toothache.

'The flutes play all night,' the strange man said, 'and the stars are as big as the moon and the moon is as big as a lake.'

As the bus started up again they slipped back into the darkness and only the thin thread of lights along the ceiling of the bus held them together, brought the back of the bus where she sat along with the front of the bus where the driver sat and the people sitting there so far away from her. The lights tied them together and the strange man next to her was saying, 'Nothing to do all day but lie under the trees.'

Inside the bus, traveling on, she was nothing; she was passing the trees and the occasional sleeping houses, and she was in the bus but she was between here and there, joined tenuously to the bus driver by a thread of lights, being carried along without effort of her own.

'My name is Jim,' the strange man said.

She was so deeply asleep that she stirred uneasily without knowledge, her forehead against the window, the darkness moving along beside her.

Then again that numbing shock, and, driven awake, she said, frightened, 'What's happened?'

'It's all right,' the strange man – Jim – said immediately. 'Come along.'

She followed him out of the bus, into the same restaurant, seemingly, but when she started to sit down at the same seat at the end of the counter he took her hand and led her to a table. 'Go and wash your face,' he said. 'Come back here afterward.'

She went into the ladies' room and there was a girl standing there powdering her nose. Without turning around the girl said, 'Cost's a nickel. Leave the door fixed so's the next one won't have to pay.'

The door was wedged so it would not close, with half a match folder in the lock. She left it the same way and went back to the table where Jim was sitting.

'What do you want?' she said, and he pointed to another cup of coffee and a sandwich. 'Go ahead,' he said.

While she was eating her sandwich she heard his voice, musical and soft, 'And while we were sailing past the island we heard a voice calling us . . .'

Back in the bus Jim said, 'Put your head on my shoulder now, and go to sleep.'

'I'm all right,' she said.

'No,' Jim said. 'Before, your head was rattling against the window.'

Once more she slept, and once more the bus stopped and she woke frightened, and Jim brought her again to a restaurant and more coffee. Her tooth came alive then, and with one hand pressing her cheek she searched through the pockets of her coat and then through her pocketbook until she found the little bottle of codeine pills and she took two while Jim watched her.

She was finishing her coffee when she heard the sound of the bus motor and she started up suddenly, hurrying, and with Jim holding her arm she fled back into the dark shelter of her seat. The bus was moving forward when she realized that she had left her bottle of codeine pills sitting on the table in the restaurant and now she was at the mercy of her tooth. For a minute she stared back at the lights of the restaurant through the bus window and then she put her head on Jim's shoulder and he was saying as she fell asleep, 'The sand is so white it looks like snow, but it's hot, even at night it's hot under your feet.'

Then they stopped for the last time, and Jim brought her out of the bus and they stood for a minute in New York together. A woman passing them in the station said to the man following her with suitcases, 'We're just on time, it's five-fifteen.'

'I'm going to the dentist,' she said to Jim.

'I know,' he said. 'I'll watch out for you.'

He went away, although she did not see him go. She thought to watch for his blue suit going through the door, but there was nothing.

I ought to have thanked him, she thought stupidly, and went slowly into the station restaurant, where she ordered coffee again. The counter man looked at her with the worn sympathy of one who has spent a long night watching people get off and on buses. 'Sleepy?' he asked.

'Yes,' she said.

She discovered after a while that the bus station joined Pennsylvania Terminal and she was able to get into the main waiting-room and find a seat on one of the benches by the time she fell asleep again.

Then someone shook her rudely by the shoulder and said, 'What train you taking, lady, it's nearly seven.' She sat up and saw her pocketbook on her lap, her feet neatly crossed, a clock glaring into her face. She said, 'Thank you,' and got up and walked blindly past the benches and got on to the escalator. Someone got on immediately behind her and touched her arm; she turned and it was Jim. 'The grass is so green and so soft,' he said, smiling, 'and the water of the river is so cool.'

She stared at him tiredly. When the escalator reached the top she stepped off and started to walk to the street she saw ahead. Jim came along beside her and his voice went on, 'The sky is bluer than anything you've ever seen, and the songs . . .'

She stepped quickly away from him and thought that people were looking at her as they passed. She stood on the corner waiting for the light to change and Jim came swiftly up to her and then away. 'Look,' he said as he passed, and he held out a handful of pearls.

Across the street there was a restaurant, just opening. She went in and sat down at a table, and a waitress was standing beside her frowning. 'You was asleep,' the waitress said accusingly.

'I'm very sorry,' she said. It was morning. 'Poached eggs and coffee, please.'

It was a quarter to eight when she left the restaurant, and she thought, if I take a bus, and go straight downtown now, I can sit in the drugstore across the street from the dentist's office and have more coffee until about eight-thirty and then go into the dentist's when it opens and he can take me first.

The buses were beginning to fill up; she got into the first bus that came along and could not find a seat. She wanted to go to Twenty-third Street, and got a seat just as they were passing Twenty-sixth Street; when she woke she was so far downtown that it took her nearly half-an-hour to find a bus and get back to Twenty-third.

At the corner of Twenty-third Street, while she was waiting for the light to change, she was caught up in a crowd of people, and when they crossed the street and separated to go in different directions someone fell into step beside her. For a minute she walked on without looking up, staring resentfully at the sidewalk, her tooth burning her, and then she looked up, but there was no blue suit among the people pressing by on either side.

When she turned into the office building where her dentist was, it was still very early morning. The doorman in the office building was freshly shaven and his hair was combed; he held the door open briskly, as at five o'clock he would be sluggish, his hair faintly out of place. She went in through the door with a feeling of achievement; she had come successfully from one place to another, and this was the end of her journey and her objective.

The clean white nurse sat at the desk in the office; her eyes took in the swollen cheek, the tired shoulders, and she said, 'You poor thing, you look worn out.'

'I have a toothache.' The nurse half-smiled, as though she were still waiting for the day when someone would come in and say, 'My feet hurt.' She stood up into the professional sunlight. 'Come right in,' she said. 'We won't make you wait.'

There was sunlight on the headrest of the dentist's chair, on the round white table, on the drill bending its smooth chromium head. The dentist smiled with the same tolerance as the nurse; perhaps all human ailments were contained in the teeth, and he could fix them if people would only come to him in time. The nurse said smoothly, 'I'll get her file, doctor. We thought we'd better bring her right in.'

She felt, while they were taking an X-ray, that there was nothing in her head to stop the malicious eye of the camera, as though the camera would look through her and photograph the nails in the wall next to her, or the dentist's cuff buttons, or the small thin bones of the dentist's instruments; the dentist said, 'Extraction,' regretfully to the nurse, and the nurse said, 'Yes, doctor, I'll call them right away.'

Her tooth, which had brought her here unerringly, seemed now the only part of her to have any identity. It seemed to have had its picture taken without her; it was the important creature which must be recorded and examined and gratified; she was only its unwilling vehicle, and only as such was she of interest to the dentist and the nurse, only as the bearer of her tooth was she worth their immediate and practised attention. The dentist handed her a slip of paper with the picture of a full set of teeth drawn on it; her living tooth was checked with a black mark, and across the top of the paper was written 'Lower molar; extraction.'

'Take this slip,' the dentist said, 'and go right up to the address on this card; it's a surgeon dentist. They'll take care of you there.'

'What will they do?' she said. Not the question she wanted to ask, not: What about me? or, How far down do the roots go?

'They'll take that tooth out,' the dentist said testily, turning away. 'Should have been done years ago.'

I've stayed too long, she thought, he's tired of my tooth. She got up out of the dentist's chair and said, 'Thank you. Good-bye.'

'Good-bye,' the dentist said. At the last minute he smiled at her, showing her his full white teeth, all in perfect control.

'Are you all right? Does it bother you too much?' the nurse asked.

'I'm all right.'

'I can give you some codeine tablets,' the nurse said. 'We'd rather you didn't take anything right now, of course, but I think I could let you have them if the tooth is really bad.'

'No,' she said, remembering her little bottle of codeine pills on the table of a restaurant between here and there. 'No, it doesn't bother me too much.'

'Well,' the nurse said, 'good luck.'

She went down the stairs and out past the doorman; in the fifteen minutes she had been upstairs he had lost a little of his pristine morningness, and his bow was just a fraction smaller than before.

'Taxi?' he asked, and, remembering the bus down to Twenty-third Street, she said, 'Yes.'

Just as the doorman came back from the curb, bowing to the taxi he seemed to believe he had invented, she thought a hand waved to her from the crowd across the street.

She read the address on the card the dentist had given her and repeated it carefully to the taxi driver. With the card and the little slip of paper with 'Lower molar' written on it and her tooth identified so clearly, she sat without moving, her hands still around the papers, her eyes almost closed. She thought she must have been asleep again when the taxi stopped suddenly, and the driver, reaching around to open the door, said, 'Here we are, lady.' He looked at her curiously.

'I'm going to have a tooth pulled,' she said.

'Jesus,' the taxi driver said. She paid him and he said, 'Good luck,' as he slammed the door.

This was a strange building, the entrance flanked by medical signs carved in stone; the doorman here was faintly professional, as though he were competent to prescribe if she did not care to go any farther. She went past him, going straight ahead until an elevator opened its door to her. In the elevator she showed the elevator man the card and he said, 'Seventh floor.'

She had to back up in the elevator for a nurse to wheel in an old lady in a wheelchair. The old lady was calm and restful, sitting there in the elevator with a rug over her knees; she said, 'Nice day' to the elevator operator and he said, 'Good to see the sun,' and then the old lady lay back in her chair and the nurse straightened the rug around her knees and said, 'Now we're not going to worry,' and the old lady said irritably, 'Who's worrying?'

They got out at the fourth floor. The elevator went on up and then the operator said, 'Seven,' and the elevator stopped and the door opened.

'Straight down the hall and to your left,' the operator said.

There were closed doors on either side of the hall. Some of them said 'DDS,' some of them said 'Clinic,' some of them said 'X-Ray.' One of them, looking wholesome and friendly and somehow most comprehensible, said 'Ladies.' Then she turned to the left and found a door with the name on the card and she opened it and went in. There was a nurse sitting behind a glass window, almost as in a bank, and potted palms in tubs in the corners of the waiting-room, and new magazines and comfortable chairs. The nurse behind the glass window said, 'Yes?' as though you had overdrawn your account with the dentist and were two teeth in arrears.

She handed her slip of paper through the glass window and the nurse looked at it and said, 'Lower molar, yes. They called about you. Will you come right in, please? Through the door to your left.'

Into the vault? she almost said, and then silently opened the door and went in. Another nurse was waiting, and she smiled and turned, expecting to be followed, with no visible doubt about her right to lead.

There was another X-ray, and the nurse told another nurse: 'Lower molar,' and the other nurse said, 'Come this way, please.'

There were labyrinths and passages, seeming to lead into the heart of the office building, and she was put, finally, in a cubicle where there was a couch with a pillow and a wash-basin and a chair.

'Wait here,' the nurse said. 'Relax if you can.'

'I'll probably go to sleep,' she said.

'Fine,' the nurse said. 'You won't have to wait long.'

She waited, probably for over an hour, although she spent the time half-sleeping, waking only when someone passed the door; occasionally the nurse looked in and smiled, once she said, 'Won't have to wait much longer.' Then, suddenly, the nurse was back, no longer smiling, no longer the good hostess, but efficient and hurried. 'Come along,' she said, and moved purpose-fully out of the little room into the hallways again.

Then, quickly, more quickly than she was able to see, she was sitting in the chair and there was a towel around her head and a towel under her chin and the nurse was leaning a hand on her shoulder.

'Will it hurt?' she asked.

'No,' the nurse said, smiling. 'You know it won't hurt, don't you?'

'Yes,' she said.

The dentist came in and smiled down on her from over her head. 'Well,' he said.

'Will it hurt?' she said.

'Now,' he said cheerfully, 'we couldn't stay in busi-ness if we hurt people.' All the time he talked he was busying himself with metal hidden under a towel, and great machinery being wheeled in almost silently behind her. 'We couldn't stay in business at all,' he said. 'All you've got to worry about is telling us all your secrets while you're asleep. Want to watch out for that, you know. Lower molar?' he said to the nurse.

'Lower molar, doctor,' she said.

Then they put the metal-tasting rubber mask over her face and the dentist said, 'You know,' two or three times absent-mindedly while she could still see him over the mask. The nurse said, 'Relax your hands, dear,' and after a long time she felt her fingers relaxing.

First of all things get so far away, she thought, remember this. And remember the metallic sound and taste of all of it. And the outrage.

And then the whirling music, the ringing confusedly loud music that went on and on, around and around, and she was running as fast as she could down a long horribly clear hallway with doors on both sides and at the end of the hallway was Jim, holding out his hands and laughing, and calling something she could never hear because of the loud music, and she was running and then she said, 'I'm not afraid,' and someone from the door next to her took her arm and pulled her through and the world widened alarmingly until it would never stop and then it stopped with the head of the dentist looking down at her and the window dropped into place in front of her and the nurse was holding her arm.

'Why did you pull me back?' she said, and her mouth was full of blood. 'I wanted to go on.'

'I didn't pull you,' the nurse said, but the dentist said, 'She's not out of it yet.'

She began to cry without moving and felt the tears rolling down her face and the nurse wiped them off with a towel. There was no blood anywhere around except in her mouth; everything was as clean as before. The dentist was gone, suddenly, and the nurse put out her arm and helped her out of the chair. 'Did I talk?' she asked suddenly, anxiously. 'Did I say anything?'

'You said, "I'm not afraid,"' the nurse said soothingly. 'Just as you were coming out of it.'

'No,' she said, stopping to pull at the arm around her. 'Did I *say* anything? Did I say where he is?'

'You didn't say *anything*,' the nurse said. 'The doctor was only teasing you.'

'Where's my tooth?' she asked suddenly, and the nurse laughed and said, 'All gone. Never bother you again.'

She was back in the cubicle, and she lay down on the couch and cried, and the nurse brought her whisky in a paper cup and set it on the edge of the wash-basin.

'God has given me blood to drink,' she said to the nurse, and the nurse said, 'Don't rinse your mouth or it won't clot.'

After a long time the nurse came back and said to her from the doorway, smiling, 'I see you're awake again.'

'Why?' she said.

'You've been asleep,' the nurse said. 'I didn't want to wake you.'

She sat up; she was dizzy and it seemed that she had been in the cubicle all her life.

'Do you want to come along now?' the nurse said, all kindness again. She held out the same arm, strong enough to guide any wavering footstep; this time they went back through the long corridor to where the nurse sat behind the bank window.

'All through?' this nurse said brightly. 'Sit down a minute, then.' She indicated a chair next to the glass window, and turned away to write busily. 'Do not rinse your mouth for two hours,' she said, without turning around. 'Take a laxative tonight, take two aspirin if there is any pain. If there is much pain or excessive bleeding, notify this office at once. All right?' she said, and smiled brightly again.

There was a new little slip of paper; this one said, 'Extraction,' and underneath, 'Do not rinse mouth. Take mild laxative. Two aspirin for pain. If pain is excessive or any hemorrhage occurs, notify office.'

'Good-bye,' the nurse said pleasantly.

'Good-bye,' she said.

With the little slip of paper in her hand, she went out through the glass door and, still almost asleep, turned the corner and started down the hall. When she opened her eyes a little and saw that it was a long hall with doorways on either side, she stopped and then saw the door marked 'Ladies' and went in. Inside there was a vast room with windows and wicker chairs and glaring white tiles and glittering silver faucets; there were four or five women around the wash-basins, combing their hair, putting on lipstick. She went directly to the nearest of the three wash-basins, took a paper towel, dropped her pocketbook and the little slip of paper on the floor next to her, and fumbled with the faucets, soaking the towel until it was dripping. Then she slapped it against her face violently. Her eyes cleared and she felt fresher, so she soaked the paper again and rubbed her face with it. She felt out blindly for another paper towel, and the woman next to her handed her one, with a laugh she could hear, although she could not see for the water in her eyes. She heard one of the women say, 'Where we going for lunch?' and another one say, 'Just downstairs, prob'ly. Old fool says I gotta be back in half-an-hour.'

Then she realized that at the wash-basin she was in the way of the women in a hurry so she dried her face quickly. It was when she stepped a little aside to let someone else get to the basin and stood up and glanced into the mirror that she realized with a slight stinging shock that she had no idea which face was hers!

She looked into the mirror as though into a group of strangers, all staring at her or around her; no one was familiar in the group, no one smiled at her or looked at her with recognition; you'd think my own face would know me, she thought, with a queer numbness in her throat. There was a creamy chinless face with bright blonde hair, and a sharp-looking face under a red veiled hat, and a colorless anxious face with brown hair pulled straight back, and a square rosy face under a square haircut, and two or three more faces pushing close to the mirror, moving, regarding themselves. Perhaps it's not a mirror, she thought, maybe it's a window and I'm looking straight through at women washing on the other side. But there were women combing their hair and consulting the mirror; the group was on her side, and she thought, I hope I'm not the blonde, and lifted her hand and put it on her cheek.

She was the pale anxious one with the hair pulled back and when she realized it she was indignant and moved hurriedly back through the crowd of women, thinking, It isn't fair, why don't I have any color in my face? There were some pretty faces there, why didn't I take one of those? I didn't have time, she told herself sullenly, they didn't give me time to think, I could have had one of the nice faces, even the blonde would be better.

She backed up and sat down in one of the wicker chairs. It's mean, she was thinking. She put her hand up and felt her hair; it was loosened after her sleep but that was definitely the way she wore it, pulled straight back all around and fastened at the back of her neck with a wide tight barrette. Like a schoolgirl, she thought, only – remembering the pale face in the mirror – only I'm older than that. She unfastened the barrette with difficulty and brought it around where she could look at it. Her hair fell softly around her face; it was warm and reached to her shoulders. The barrette was silver; engraved on it was the name, 'Clara.'

'Clara,' she said aloud. *'Clara?'* Two of the women leaving the room smiled back at her over their shoulders; almost all the women were leaving now, correctly combed and lipsticked, hurrying out talking together. In the space of a second, like birds leaving a tree, they all were gone and she sat alone in the room. She dropped the barrette into the ashstand next to her chair; the ashstand was deep and metal, and the barrette made a satisfactory clang falling down. Her hair down on her shoulders, she opened her pocketbook, and began to take things out, setting them on her lap as she did so. Handkerchief, plain, white, uninitialled. Compact, square and brown tortoise-shell plastic, with a powder compartment and a rouge compartment; the rouge compartment had obviously never been used, although the powder cake was half-gone. That's why I'm so pale, she thought, and set the compact down. Lipstick, a rose shade, almost finished. A comb, an opened package of cigarettes and a package of matches, a change purse, and a wallet. The change purse was red imitation leather with a zipper across the top; she opened it and dumped the money out into her hand. Nickels, dimes, pennies, a quarter. Ninety-seven cents. Can't go far on that, she thought, and opened the brown leather wallet; there was money in it but she looked first for papers and found nothing. The only thing in the wallet was money. She counted it; there were nineteen dollars. I can go a little farther on *that*, she thought.

There was nothing else in the pocketbook. No keys – shouldn't I have keys? she wondered – no papers, no address book, no identification. The pocketbook itself was imitation leather, light grey, and she looked down and discovered that she was wearing a dark grey flannel suit and a salmon-pink blouse with a ruffle around the neck. Her shoes were black and stout with moderate heels and they had laces, one of which was untied. She was wearing beige stockings and there was a ragged tear in the right knee and a great ragged run going down her leg and ending in a hole in the toe which she could feel inside her shoe. She was wearing a pin on the lapel of her suit which, when she turned it around to look at it, was a blue plastic letter C. She took the pin off and dropped it into the ashstand, and it made a sort of clatter at the bottom, with a metallic clang when it landed on the barrette. Her hands were small, with stubby fingers and no nail polish; she wore a thin gold wedding ring on her left hand and no other jewelry.

Sitting alone in the ladies' room in the wicker chair, she thought, The least I can do is get rid of these stockings. Since no one was around she took off her shoes and stripped away the stockings with a feeling of relief when her toe was released from the hole. Hide them, she thought: the paper towel wastebasket. When she stood up she got a better sight of herself in the mirror; it was worse than she had thought: the grey suit bagged in the seat, her legs were bony, and her shoulders sagged. I look fifty, she thought; and then, consulting the face, but I can't be more than thirty. Her hair hung down untidily around the pale face and with sudden anger she fumbled in the pocketbook and found the lipstick; she drew an emphatic rosy mouth on the pale face, realizing as she did so that she was not very expert at it, and with the red mouth the face looking at her seemed somehow better to her, so she opened the compact and put on pink cheeks with the rouge. The cheeks were uneven and patent, and the red mouth glaring, but at least the face was no longer pale and anxious.

She put the stockings into the wastebasket and went bare-legged out into the hall again, and purposefully to the elevator. The elevator operator said, 'Down?' when he saw her and she stepped in and the elevator carried her silently downstairs. She went back past the grave professional doorman and out into the street where people were passing, and she stood in front of the building and waited. After a few minutes Jim came out of a crowd of people passing and came over to her and took her hand.

Somewhere between here and there was her bottle of codeine pills, upstairs on the floor of the ladies' room she had left a little slip of paper headed 'Extraction'; seven floors below, oblivious of the people who stepped sharply along the sidewalk, not noticing their occasional curious glances, her hand in Jim's and her hair down on her shoulders, she ran barefoot through hot sand.

The Witch

The coach was so nearly empty that the little boy had a seat all to himself, and his mother sat across the aisle on the seat next to the little boy's sister, a baby with a piece of toast in one hand and a rattle in the other. She was strapped securely to the seat so she could sit up and look around, and whenever she began to slip slowly sideways the strap caught her and held her halfway until her mother turned around and straightened her again. The little boy was looking out the window and eating a cookie, and the mother was reading quietly, answering the little boy's questions without looking up.

'We're on a river,' the little boy said. 'This is a river and we're on it.'

'Fine,' his mother said.

'We're on a bridge over a river,' the little boy said to himself.

The few other people in the coach were sitting at the

other end of the car; if any of them had occasion to come down the aisle the little boy would look around and say, 'Hi,' and the stranger would usually say, 'Hi,' back and sometimes ask the little boy if he were enjoying the train ride, or even tell him he was a fine big fellow. These comments annoyed the little boy and he would turn irritably back to the window.

'There's a cow,' he would say, or, sighing, 'How far do we have to go?'

'Not much longer now,' his mother said, each time.

Once the baby, who was very quiet and busy with her rattle and her toast, which the mother would renew constantly, fell over too far sideways and banged her head. She began to cry, and for a minute there was noise and movement around the mother's seat. The little boy slid down from his own seat and ran across the aisle to pet his sister's feet and beg her not to cry, and finally the baby laughed and went back to her toast, and the little boy received a lollipop from his mother and went back to the window.

'I saw a witch,' he said to his mother after a minute. 'There was a big old ugly old bad old witch outside.'

'Fine,' his mother said.

'A big old ugly witch and I told her to go away and she went away,' the little boy went on, in a quiet narrative to himself, 'she came and said, "I'm going to eat you up," and I said, "no, you're not," and I chased her away, the bad old mean witch.'

He stopped talking and looked up as the outside door of the coach opened and a man came in. He was an elderly man, with a pleasant face under white hair; his blue suit was only faintly touched by the disarray that comes from a long train trip. He was carrying a cigar, and when the little boy said, 'Hi,' the man gestured at him with the cigar and said, 'Hello yourself, son.' He stopped just beside the little boy's seat, and leaned against the back, looking down at the little boy, who craned his neck to look upward. 'What you looking for out that window?' the man asked.

'Witches,' the little boy said promptly. 'Bad old mean witches.'

'I see,' the man said. 'Find many?'

'My father smokes cigars,' the little boy said.

'All men smoke cigars,' the man said. 'Someday you'll smoke a cigar, too.'

'I'm a man already,' the little boy said.

'How old are you?' the man asked.

The little boy, at the eternal question, looked at the man suspiciously for a minute and then said, 'Twenty-six. Eight hunnerd and forty eighty.'

His mother lifted her head from the book. 'Four,' she said, smiling fondly at the little boy.

'Is that so?' the man said politely to the little boy. 'Twenty-six.' He nodded his head at the mother across the aisle. 'Is that your mother?'

The little boy leaned forward to look and then said, 'Yes, that's her.'

'What's your name?' the man asked.

The little boy looked suspicious again. 'Mr Jesus,' he said.

'*Johnny*,' the little boy's mother said. She caught the little boy's eye and frowned deeply.

'That's my sister over there,' the little boy said to the man. 'She's twelve-and-a-half.'

'Do you love your sister?' the man asked. The little boy stared, and the man came around the side of the seat and sat down next to the little boy. 'Listen,' the man said, 'shall I tell you about my little sister?'

The mother, who had looked up anxiously when the man sat down next to her little boy, went peacefully back to her book.

'Tell me about your sister,' the little boy said. 'Was she a witch?'

'Maybe,' the man said.

The little boy laughed excitedly, and the man leaned back and puffed at his cigar. 'Once upon a time,' he began, 'I had a little sister, just like yours.' The little boy looked up at the man, nodding at every word. 'My little sister,' the man went on, 'was so pretty and so nice that I loved her more than anything else in the world. So shall I tell you what I did?'

The little boy nodded more vehemently, and the mother lifted her eyes from her book and smiled, listening.

'I bought her a rocking-horse and a doll and a million lollipops,' the man said, 'and then I took her and I put my hands around her neck and I pinched her and I pinched her until she was dead.'

The little boy gasped and the mother turned around, her smile fading. She opened her mouth, and then closed it again as the man went on, 'And then I took and I cut her head off and I took her head –'

'Did you cut her all in pieces?' the little boy asked breathlessly.

'I cut off her head and her hands and her feet and her hair and her nose,' the man said, 'and I hit her with a stick and I killed her.'

'Wait a minute,' the mother said, but the baby fell over sideways just at that minute and by the time the mother had set her up again the man was going on.

'And I took her head and I pulled out all her hair and –'

'Your little *sister*?' the little boy prompted eagerly.

'My little sister,' the man said firmly. 'And I put her head in a cage with a bear and the bear ate it all up.'

35

'Ate her *head* all up?' the little boy asked.

The mother put her book down and came across the aisle. She stood next to the man and said, 'Just what do you think you're doing?' The man looked up courteously and she said, 'Get out of here.'

'Did I frighten you?' the man said. He looked down at the little boy and nudged him with an elbow and he and the little boy laughed.

'This man cut up his little sister,' the little boy said to his mother.

'I can very easily call the conductor,' the mother said to the man.

'The conductor will *eat* my mommy,' the little boy said. 'We'll chop her head off.'

'And little sister's head, too,' the man said. He stood up, and the mother stood back to let him get out of the seat. 'Don't ever come back in this car,' she said.

'My mommy will eat *you*,' the little boy said to the man.

The man laughed, and the little boy laughed, and then the man said, 'Excuse me,' to the mother and went past her out of the car. When the door had closed behind him the little boy said, 'How much longer do we have to stay on this old train?'

'Not much longer,' the mother said. She stood looking at the little boy, wanting to say something, and finally she said, 'You sit still and be a good boy. You may have another lollipop.'

The little boy climbed down eagerly and followed his mother back to her seat. She took a lollipop from a bag in her pocketbook and gave it to him. 'What do you say?' she asked.

'Thank you,' the little boy said. 'Did that man really cut his little sister up in pieces?'

'He was just teasing,' the mother said, and added urgently, 'Just *teasing*.'

'Prob'ly,' the little boy said. With his lollipop he went back to his own seat, and settled himself to look out the window again. 'Prob'ly he was a witch.'

Charles

The day my son Laurie started kindergarten he re-
nounced corduroy overalls with bibs and began wearing
blue jeans with a belt; I watched him go off the first
morning with the older girl next door, seeing clearly that
an era of my life was ended, my sweet-voiced nursery-
school tot replaced by a long-trousered, swaggering
character who forgot to stop at the corner and wave
good-bye to me.

He came home the same way, the front door slam-
ming open, his cap on the floor, and the voice suddenly
become raucous shouting, 'Isn't anybody *here*?'

At lunch he spoke insolently to his father, spilled his
baby sister's milk, and remarked that his teacher said
we were not to take the name of the Lord in vain.

'How *was* school today?' I asked, elaborately casual.

'All right,' he said.

'Did you learn anything?' his father asked.

Laurie regarded his father coldly. 'I didn't learn nothing,' he said.

'Anything,' I said. 'Didn't learn anything.'

'The teacher spanked a boy, though,' Laurie said, addressing his bread and butter. 'For being fresh,' he added, with his mouth full.

'What did he do?' I asked. 'Who was it?'

Laurie thought. 'It was Charles,' he said. 'He was fresh. The teacher spanked him and made him stand in a corner. He was awfully fresh.'

'What did he do?' I asked again, but Laurie slid off his chair, took a cookie, and left, while his father was still saying, 'See here, young man.'

The next day Laurie remarked at lunch, as soon as he sat down, 'Well, Charles was bad again today.' He grinned enormously and said, 'Today Charles hit the teacher.'

'Good heavens,' I said, mindful of the Lord's name, 'I suppose he got spanked again?'

'He sure did,' Laurie said. 'Look up,' he said to his father.

'What?' his father said, looking up.

'Look down,' Laurie said. 'Look at my thumb. Gee, you're dumb.' He began to laugh insanely.

'Why did Charles hit the teacher?' I asked quickly.

'Because she tried to make him color with red crayons,' Laurie said. 'Charles wanted to color with green crayons so he hit the teacher and she spanked him and said no-body play with Charles but everybody did.'

The third day – it was Wednesday of the first week – Charles bounced a see-saw on to the head of a little girl and made her bleed, and the teacher made him stay inside all during recess. Thursday Charles had to stand in a corner during story-time because he kept pounding his feet on the floor. Friday Charles was deprived of blackboard privileges because he threw chalk.

On Saturday I remarked to my husband, 'Do you think kindergarten is too unsettling for Laurie? All this toughness, and bad grammar, and this Charles boy sounds like such a bad influence.'

'It'll be all right,' my husband said reassuringly. 'Bound to be people like Charles in the world. Might as well meet them now as later.'

On Monday Laurie came home late, full of news. 'Charles,' he shouted as he came up the hill; I was waiting anxiously on the front steps. 'Charles,' Laurie yelled all the way up the hill, 'Charles was bad again.'

'Come right in,' I said, as soon as he came close enough. 'Lunch is waiting.'

'You know what Charles did?' he demanded, follow-ing me through the door. 'Charles yelled so in school they sent a boy in from first grade to tell the teacher she had to make Charles keep quiet, and so Charles had to stay after school. And so all the children stayed to watch him.'

'What did he do?' I asked.

'He just sat there,' Laurie said, climbing into his chair at the table. 'Hi, Pop, y'old dust mop.'

'Charles had to stay after school today,' I told my husband. 'Everyone stayed with him.'

'What does this Charles look like?' my husband asked Laurie. 'What's his other name?'

'He's bigger than me,' Laurie said. 'And he doesn't have any rubbers and he doesn't ever wear a jacket.'

Monday night was the first Parent–Teachers meeting, and only the fact that the baby had a cold kept me from going; I wanted passionately to meet Charles's mother. On Tuesday Laurie remarked suddenly, 'Our teacher had a friend come to see her in school today.'

'Charles's mother?' my husband and I asked simultaneously.

'Naaah,' Laurie said scornfully. 'It was a man who came and made us do exercises, we had to touch our toes. Look.' He climbed down from his chair and squatted down and touched his toes. 'Like this,' he said. He got solemnly back into his chair and said, picking up his fork, 'Charles didn't even *do* exercises.'

'That's fine,' I said heartily. 'Didn't Charles want to do exercises?'

'Naaah,' Laurie said. 'Charles was so fresh to the teacher's friend he wasn't *let* do exercises.'

'Fresh again?' I said.

'He kicked the teacher's friend,' Laurie said. 'The teacher's friend told Charles to touch his toes like I just did and Charles kicked him.'

'What are they going to do about Charles, do you suppose?' Laurie's father asked him.

Laurie shrugged elaborately. 'Throw him out of school, I guess,' he said.

Wednesday and Thursday were routine; Charles yelled during story hour and hit a boy in the stomach and made him cry. On Friday Charles stayed after school again and so did all the other children.

With the third week of kindergarten Charles was an institution in our family; the baby was being a Charles when she cried all afternoon; Laurie did a Charles when he filled his wagon full of mud and pulled it through the kitchen; even my husband, when he caught his elbow in the telephone cord and pulled telephone, ashtray, and a bowl of flowers off the table, said, after the first minute, 'Looks like Charles.'

During the third and fourth weeks it looked like a reformation in Charles; Laurie reported grimly at lunch on Thursday of the third week, 'Charles was so good today the teacher gave him an apple.'

'What?' I said, and my husband added warily, 'You mean Charles?'

'Charles,' Laurie said. 'He gave the crayons around and he picked up the books afterward and the teacher said he was her helper.'

'What happened?' I asked incredulously.

'He was her helper, that's all,' Laurie said, and shrugged.

'Can this be true, about Charles?' I asked my husband that night. 'Can something like this happen?'

'Wait and see,' my husband said cynically. 'When you've got a Charles to deal with, this may mean he's only plotting.'

He seemed to be wrong. For over a week Charles was the teacher's helper; each day he handed things out and he picked things up; no one had to stay after school.

'The P.T.A. meeting's next week again,' I told my husband one evening. 'I'm going to find Charles's mother there.'

'Ask her what happened to Charles,' my husband said. 'I'd like to know.'

'I'd like to know myself,' I said.

On Friday of that week things were back to normal. 'You know what Charles did today?' Laurie demanded at the lunch table, in a voice slightly awed. 'He told a little girl to say a word and she said it and the teacher washed her mouth out with soap and Charles laughed.'

'What word?' his father asked unwisely, and Laurie said, 'I'll have to whisper it to you, it's so bad.' He got down off his chair and went around to his father. His father bent his head down and Laurie whispered joyfully. His father's eyes widened.

'Did Charles tell the little girl to say *that*?' he asked respectfully.

'She said it *twice*,' Laurie said. 'Charles told her to say it *twice*.'

'What happened to Charles?' my husband asked.

'Nothing,' Laurie said. 'He was passing out the crayons.'

Monday morning Charles abandoned the little girl and said the evil word himself three or four times, getting his mouth washed out with soap each time. He also threw chalk.

My husband came to the door with me that evening as I set out for the P.T.A. meeting. 'Invite her over for a cup of tea after the meeting,' he said. 'I want to get a look at her.'

'If only she's there,' I said prayerfully.

'She'll be there,' my husband said. 'I don't see how they could hold a P.T.A. meeting without Charles's mother.'

Shirley Jackson

At the meeting I sat restlessly, scanning each comfortable matronly face, trying to determine which one hid the secret of Charles. None of them looked to me haggard enough. No one stood up in the meeting and apologized for the way her son had been acting. No one mentioned Charles.

After the meeting I identified and sought out Laurie's kindergarten teacher. She had a plate with a cup of tea and a piece of chocolate cake; I had a plate with a cup of tea and a piece of marshmallow cake. We maneuvered up to one another cautiously, and smiled.

'I've been so anxious to meet you,' I said. 'I'm Laurie's mother.'

'We're all so interested in Laurie,' she said.

'Well, he certainly likes kindergarten,' I said. 'He talks about it all the time.'

'We had a little trouble adjusting, the first week or so,' she said primly, 'but now he's a fine little helper. With occasional lapses, of course.'

'Laurie usually adjusts very quickly,' I said. 'I suppose this time it's Charles's influence.'

'Charles?'

'Yes,' I said, laughing, 'you must have your hands full in that kindergarten, with Charles.'

'Charles?' she said. 'We don't have any Charles in the kindergarten.'

The Lottery

The morning of June 27th was clear and sunny, with the fresh warmth of a full-summer day; the flowers were blossoming profusely and the grass was richly green. The people of the village began to gather in the square, between the post office and the bank, around ten o'clock; in some towns there were so many people that the lottery took two days and had to be started on June 26th, but in this village, where there were only about three hundred people, the whole lottery took less than two hours, so it could begin at ten o'clock in the morning and still be through in time to allow the villagers to get home for noon dinner.

The children assembled first, of course. School was recently over for the summer, and the feeling of liberty sat uneasily on most of them; they tended to gather together quietly for a while before they broke into boisterous play, and their talk was still of the classroom and the teacher, of books and reprimands. Bobby Martin had already stuffed his pockets full of stones, and the other boys soon followed his example, selecting the smoothest and roundest stones; Bobby and Harry Jones and Dickie Delacroix – the villagers pronounced this name 'Dellacroy' – eventually made a great pile of stones in one corner of the square and guarded it against the raids of the other boys. The girls stood aside, talking among themselves, looking over their shoulders at the boys, and the very small children rolled in the dust or clung to the hands of their older brothers or sisters.

Soon the men began to gather, surveying their own children, speaking of planting and rain, tractors and taxes. They stood together, away from the pile of stones in the corner, and their jokes were quiet and they smiled rather than laughed. The women, wearing faded house dresses and sweaters, came shortly after their menfolk. They greeted one another and exchanged bits of gossip as they went to join their husbands. Soon the women, standing by their husbands, began to call to their children, and the children came reluctantly, having to be called four or five times. Bobby Martin ducked under his mother's grasping hand and ran, laughing, back to the pile of stones. His father spoke up sharply, and Bobby came quickly and took his place between his father and his oldest brother.

The lottery was conducted – as were the square dances, the teen-age club, the Halloween program – by Mr Summers, who had time and energy to devote to civic activities. He was a round-faced, jovial man and he ran the coal business, and people were sorry for him, because he had no children and his wife was a scold. When he arrived in the square, carrying the black wooden box, there was a murmur of conversation among the villagers, and he waved and called, 'Little late today, folks.' The postmaster, Mr Graves, followed him, carrying a three-legged stool, and the stool was put in the center of the square and Mr Summers set the black box down on it. The villagers kept their distance, leaving a space between themselves and the stool, and when Mr Summers said, 'Some of you fellows want to give me a hand?' there was a hesitation before two men, Mr Martin and his oldest son, Baxter, came forward to hold the box steady on the stool while Mr Summers stirred up the papers inside it.

The original paraphernalia for the lottery had been lost long ago, and the black box now resting on the stool had been put into use even before Old Man Warner, the oldest man in town, was born. Mr Summers spoke frequently to the villagers about making a new box, but no one liked to upset even as much tradition as was represented by the black box. There was a story that the present box had been made with some pieces of the box that had preceded it, the one that had been constructed when the first people settled down to make a village here. Every year, after the lottery, Mr Summers began talking again about a new box, but every year the subject was allowed to fade off without anything's being done. The black box grew shabbier each year; by now it was no longer completely black but splintered badly along one side to show the original wood color, and in some places faded or stained.

Mr Martin and his oldest son, Baxter, held the black box securely on the stool until Mr Summers had stirred the papers thoroughly with his hand. Because so much of the ritual had been forgotten or discarded, Mr Summers had been successful in having slips of paper substituted for the chips of wood that had been used for generations. Chips of wood, Mr Summers had argued, had been all very well when the village was tiny, but now that the population was more than three hundred and likely to keep on growing, it was necessary to use something that would fit more easily into the black box. The night before the lottery, Mr Summers and Mr Graves made up the slips of paper and put them in the box, and it was then taken to the safe of Mr Summers' coal company and locked up until Mr Summers was ready to take it to the square next morning. The rest of the year, the box was put away, sometimes one place, sometimes another; it had spent one year in Mr Graves's barn and another year underfoot in the post office, and sometimes it was set on a shelf in the Martin grocery and left there.

There was a great deal of fussing to be done before Mr Summers declared the lottery open. There were the lists to make up – of heads of families, heads of households in each family, members of each household in each family. There was the proper swearing-in of Mr Summers by the postmaster, as the official of the lottery; at one time, some people remembered, there had been a recital of some sort, performed by the official of the lottery, a perfunctory, tuneless chant that had been rattled off duly each year; some people believed that the official of the lottery used to stand just so when he said or sang it, others believed that he was supposed to walk among the people, but years and years ago this part of the ritual had been allowed to lapse. There had been, also, a ritual salute, which the official of the lottery had had to use in addressing each person who came up to draw from the box, but this also had changed with time, until now it was felt necessary only for the official to speak to each person approaching. Mr Summers was very good at all this; in his clean white shirt and blue jeans, with one hand resting carelessly on the black box, he seemed very proper and important as he talked interminably to Mr Graves and the Martins.

Just as Mr Summers finally left off talking and turned to the assembled villagers, Mrs Hutchinson came hurriedly along the path to the square, her sweater thrown over her shoulders, and slid into place in the back of the crowd. 'Clean forgot what day it was,' she said to Mrs Delacroix, who stood next to her, and they both laughed softly. 'Thought my old man was out back stacking wood,' Mrs Hutchinson went on, 'and then I looked out the window and the kids was gone, and then I remembered it was the twenty-seventh and came a-running.' She dried her hands on her apron, and Mrs Delacroix said, 'You're in time, though. They're still talking away up there.'

Mrs Hutchinson craned her neck to see through the crowd and found her husband and children standing near the front. She tapped Mrs Delacroix on the arm as a farewell and began to make her way through the crowd. The people separated good-humoredly to let her through; two or three people said, in voices just loud enough to be heard across the crowd, 'Here comes your Missus, Hutchinson,' and 'Bill, she made it after all.' Mrs Hutchinson reached her husband, and Mr Summers, who had been waiting, said cheerfully, 'Thought we were going to have to get on without you, Tessie.'

Mrs Hutchinson said, grinning, 'Wouldn't have me leave m'dishes in the sink, now, would you, Joe?' and soft laughter ran through the crowd as the people stirred back into position after Mrs Hutchinson's arrival.

'Well, now,' Mr Summers said soberly, 'guess we better get started, get this over with, so's we can go back to work. Anybody ain't here?'

'Dunbar,' several people said. 'Dunbar, Dunbar.'

Mr Summers consulted his list. 'Clyde Dunbar,' he said. 'That's right. He's broke his leg, hasn't he? Who's drawing for him?'

'Me, I guess,' a woman said, and Mr Summers turned to look at her. 'Wife draws for her husband,' Mr Summers said. 'Don't you have a grown boy to do it for you, Janey?' Although Mr Summers and everyone else in the village knew the answer perfectly well, it was the business of the official of the lottery to ask such questions formally. Mr Summers waited with an expression of polite interest while Mrs Dunbar answered.

'Horace's not but sixteen yet,' Mrs Dunbar said regretfully. 'Guess I gotta fill in for the old man this year.'

'Right,' Mr Summers said. He made a note on the list he was holding. Then he asked, 'Watson boy drawing this year?'

A tall boy in the crowd raised his hand. 'Here,' he said. 'I'm drawing for m'mother and me.' He blinked his eyes nervously and ducked his head as several voices in the crowd said things like 'Good fellow, Jack,' and 'Glad to see your mother's got a man to do it.'

'Well,' Mr Summers said, 'guess that's everyone. Old Man Warner make it?'

'Here,' a voice said, and Mr Summers nodded.

A sudden hush fell on the crowd as Mr Summers cleared his throat and looked at the list. 'All ready?' he called. 'Now, I'll read the names – heads of families first – and the men come up and take a paper out of the box. Keep the paper folded in your hand without looking at it until everyone has had a turn. Everything clear?'

The people had done it so many times that they only half-listened to the directions; most of them were quiet, wetting their lips, not looking around. Then Mr Summers raised one hand high and said, 'Adams.' A man disengaged himself from the crowd and came forward. 'Hi, Steve,' Mr Summers said, and Mr Adams said, 'Hi, Joe.' They grinned at one another humorlessly and nervously. Then Mr Adams reached into the black box and took out a folded paper. He held it firmly by one corner as he turned and went hastily back to his place in the crowd, where he stood a little apart from his family, not looking down at his hand.

'Allen,' Mr Summers said. 'Anderson . . . Bentham.'

'Seems like there's no time at all between lotteries any more,' Mrs Delacroix said to Mrs Graves in the back row. 'Seems like we got through with the last one only last week.'

'Time sure goes fast,' Mrs Graves said.

'Clark . . . Delacroix.'

'There goes my old man,' Mrs Delacroix said. She held her breath while her husband went forward.

'Dunbar,' Mr Summers said, and Mrs Dunbar went steadily to the box while one of the women said, 'Go on, Janey,' and another said, 'There she goes.'

'We're next,' Mrs Graves said. She watched while Mr Graves came around from the side of the box, greeted Mr Summers gravely, and selected a slip of paper from the box. By now, all through the crowd there were men holding the small folded papers in their large hands, turning them over and over nervously. Mrs Dunbar and her two sons stood together, Mrs Dunbar holding the slip of paper.

'Harburt . . . Hutchinson.'

'Get up there, Bill,' Mrs Hutchinson said, and the people near her laughed.

'Jones.'

'They do say,' Mr Adams said to Old Man Warner, who stood next to him, 'that over in the north village they're talking of giving up the lottery.'

Old Man Warner snorted. 'Pack of crazy fools,' he said. 'Listening to the young folks, nothing's good enough for *them*. Next thing you know, they'll be wanting to go back to living in caves, nobody work any more, live *that* way for a while. Used to be a saying about "Lottery in June, corn be heavy soon." First thing you know, we'd all be eating stewed chickweed and acorns. There's *always* been a lottery,' he added petulantly. 'Bad enough to see young Joe Summers up there joking with everybody.'

'Some places have already quit lotteries,' Mrs Adams said.

'Nothing but trouble in *that*,' Old Man Warner said stoutly. 'Pack of young fools.'

'Martin.' And Bobby Martin watched his father go forward. 'Overdyke . . . Percy.'

'I wish they'd hurry,' Mrs Dunbar said to her older son. 'I wish they'd hurry.'

'They're almost through,' her son said.

'You get ready to run tell Dad,' Mrs Dunbar said.

Mr Summers called his own name and then stepped forward precisely and selected a slip from the box. Then he called, 'Warner.'

'Seventy-seventh year I been in the lottery,' Old Man Warner said as he went through the crowd. 'Seventy-seventh time.'

'Watson.' The tall boy came awkwardly through the crowd. Someone said, 'Don't be nervous, Jack,' and Mr Summers said, 'Take your time, son.'

'Zanini.'

After that, there was a long pause, a breathless pause, until Mr Summers, holding his slip of paper in the air, said, 'All right, fellows.' For a minute, no one moved, and then all the slips of paper were opened. Suddenly, all the women began to speak at once, saying, 'Who is it?' 'Who's got it?' 'Is it the Dunbars?' 'Is it the Watsons?' Then the voices began to say, 'It's Hutchinson. It's Bill,' 'Bill Hutchinson's got it.'

'Go tell your father,' Mrs Dunbar said to her older son.

People began to look around to see the Hutchinsons. Bill Hutchinson was standing quiet, staring down at the paper in his hand. Suddenly, Tessie Hutchinson shouted to Mr Summers, 'You didn't give him time enough to take any paper he wanted. I saw you. It wasn't fair!'

'Be a good sport, Tessie,' Mrs Delacroix called, and Mrs Graves said, 'All of us took the same chance.'

'Shut up, Tessie,' Bill Hutchinson said.

'Well, everyone,' Mr Summers said, 'that was done pretty fast, and now we've got to be hurrying a little more to get done in time.' He consulted his next list.

Shirley Jackson

'Bill,' he said, 'you draw for the Hutchinson family. You got any other households in the Hutchinsons?'

'There's Don and Eva,' Mrs Hutchinson yelled. 'Make *them* take their chance!'

'Daughters draw with their husbands' families, Tessie,' Mr Summers said gently. 'You know that as well as anyone else.'

'It wasn't *fair*,' Tessie said.

'I guess not, Joe,' Bill Hutchinson said regretfully. 'My daughter draws with her husband's family, that's only fair. And I've got no other family except the kids.'

'Then, as far as drawing for families is concerned, it's you,' Mr Summers said in explanation, 'and as far as drawing for households is concerned, that's you, too. Right?'

'Right,' Bill Hutchinson said.

'How many kids, Bill?' Mr Summers asked formally.

'Three,' Bill Hutchinson said. 'There's Bill, Jr, and Nancy, and little Dave. And Tessie and me.'

'All right, then,' Mr Summers said. 'Harry, you got their tickets back?'

Mr Graves nodded and held up the slips of paper. 'Put them in the box, then,' Mr Summers directed. 'Take Bill's and put it in.'

'I think we ought to start over,' Mrs Hutchinson

58

said, as quietly as she could. 'I tell you it wasn't *fair*. You didn't give him time enough to choose. *Every*body saw that.'

Mr Graves had selected the five slips and put them in the box, and he dropped all the papers but those onto the ground, where the breeze caught them and lifted them off.

'Listen, everybody,' Mrs Hutchinson was saying to the people around her.

'Ready, Bill?' Mr Summers asked, and Bill Hutchinson, with one quick glance around at his wife and children, nodded.

'Remember,' Mr Summers said, 'take the slips and keep them folded until each person has taken one. Harry, you help little Dave.' Mr Graves took the hand of the little boy, who came willingly with him up to the box. 'Take a paper out of the box, Davy,' Mr Summers said. Davy put his hand into the box and laughed. 'Take just *one* paper,' Mr Summers said. 'Harry, you hold it for him.' Mr Graves took the child's hand and removed the folded paper from the tight fist and held it while little Dave stood next to him and looked up at him wonderingly.

'Nancy next,' Mr Summers said. Nancy was twelve, and her school friends breathed heavily as she went forward, switching her skirt, and took a slip daintily from the box. 'Bill, Jr,' Mr Summers said, and Billy, his face red and his feet overlarge, nearly knocked the box over as he got a paper out. 'Tessie,' Mr Summers said. She hesitated for a minute, looking around defiantly, and then set her lips and went up to the box. She snatched a paper out and held it behind her.

'Bill,' Mr Summers said, and Bill Hutchinson reached into the box and felt around, bringing his hand out at last with the slip of paper in it.

The crowd was quiet. A girl whispered, 'I hope it's not Nancy,' and the sound of the whisper reached the edges of the crowd.

'It's not the way it used to be,' Old Man Warner said clearly. 'People ain't the way they used to be.'

'All right,' Mr Summers said. 'Open the papers. Harry, you open little Dave's.'

Mr Graves opened the slip of paper and there was a general sigh through the crowd as he held it up and everyone could see that it was blank. Nancy and Bill, Jr, opened theirs at the same time, and both beamed and laughed, turning around to the crowd and holding their slips of paper above their heads.

'Tessie,' Mr Summers said. There was a pause, and then Mr Summers looked at Bill Hutchinson, and Bill unfolded his paper and showed it. It was blank.

'It's Tessie,' Mr Summers said, and his voice was hushed. 'Show us her paper, Bill.'

Bill Hutchinson went over to his wife and forced the slip of paper out of her hand. It had a black spot on it, the black spot Mr Summers had made the night before with the heavy pencil in the coal-company office. Bill Hutchinson held it up, and there was a stir in the crowd.

'All right, folks,' Mr Summers said. 'Let's finish quickly.'

Although the villagers had forgotten the ritual and lost the original black box, they still remembered to use stones. The pile of stones the boys had made earlier was ready; there were stones on the ground with the blowing scraps of paper that had come out of the box. Mrs Delacroix selected a stone so large she had to pick it up with both hands and turned to Mrs Dunbar. 'Come on,' she said. 'Hurry up.'

Mrs Dunbar had small stones in both hands, and she said, gasping for breath, 'I can't run at all. You'll have to go ahead and I'll catch up with you.'

The children had stones already, and someone gave little Davy Hutchinson a few pebbles.

Tessie Hutchinson was in the center of a cleared space by now, and she held her hands out desperately as the villagers moved in on her. 'It isn't fair,' she said. A stone hit her on the side of the head.

Shirley Jackson

Old Man Warner was saying, 'Come on, come on, everyone.' Steve Adams was in the front of the crowd of villagers, with Mrs Graves beside him.

'It isn't fair, it isn't right,' Mrs Hutchinson screamed, and then they were upon her.

The Intoxicated

He was just tight enough and just familiar enough with the house to be able to go out into the kitchen alone, apparently to get ice, but actually to sober up a little; he was not quite enough a friend of the family to pass out on the living-room couch. He left the party behind without reluctance, the group by the piano singing 'Stardust,' his hostess talking earnestly to a young man with thin clean glasses and a sullen mouth; he walked guardedly through the dining-room where a little group of four or five people sat on the stiff chairs reasoning something out carefully among themselves; the kitchen doors swung abruptly to his touch, and he sat down beside a white enamel table, clean and cold under his hand. He put his glass on a good spot in the green pattern and looked up to find that a young girl was regarding him speculatively from across the table.

'Hello,' he said. 'You the daughter?'

'I'm Eileen,' she said. 'Yes.'

She seemed to him baggy and ill-formed; it's the clothes they wear now, young girls, he thought foggily; her hair was braided down either side of her face, and she looked young and fresh and not dressed-up; her sweater was purplish and her hair was dark. 'You sound nice and sober,' he said, realizing that it was the wrong thing to say to young girls.

'I was just having a cup of coffee,' she said. 'May I get you one?'

He almost laughed, thinking that she expected she was dealing knowingly and competently with a rude drunk. 'Thank you,' he said, 'I believe I will.' He made an effort to focus his eyes; the coffee was hot, and when she put a cup in front of him, saying, 'I suppose you'd like it black,' he put his face into the steam and let it go into his eyes, hoping to clear his head.

'It sounds like a lovely party,' she said without longing, 'everyone must be having a fine time.'

'It is a lovely party.' He began to drink the coffee, scalding hot, wanting her to know she had helped him. His head steadied, and he smiled at her. 'I feel better,' he said, 'thanks to you.'

'It must be very warm in the other room,' she said soothingly.

Then he did laugh out loud and she frowned, but he

could see her excusing him as she went on, 'It was so hot upstairs I thought I'd like to come down for a while and sit out here.'

'Were you asleep?' he asked. 'Did we wake you?'

'I was doing my homework,' she said.

He looked at her again, seeing her against a background of careful penmanship and themes, worn textbooks and laughter between desks. 'You're in high school?'

'I'm a Senior.' She seemed to wait for him to say something, and then she said, 'I was out a year when I had pneumonia.'

He found it difficult to think of something to say (ask her about boys? basketball?), and so he pretended he was listening to the distant noises from the front of the house. 'It's a fine party,' he said again, vaguely.

'I suppose you like parties,' she said.

Dumbfounded, he sat staring into his empty coffee cup. He supposed he did like parties; her tone had been faintly surprised, as though next he were to declare for an arena with gladiators fighting wild beasts, or the solitary circular waltzing of a madman in a garden. I'm almost twice your age, my girl, he thought, but it's not so long since I did homework too. 'Play basketball?' he asked.

'No,' she said.

He felt with irritation that she had been in the kitchen first, that she lived in the house, that he must keep on talking to her. 'What's your homework about?' he asked.

'I'm writing a paper on the future of the world,' she said, and smiled. 'It sounds silly, doesn't it? I think it's silly.'

'Your party out front is talking about it. That's one reason I came out here.' He could see her thinking that that was not at all the reason he came out here, and he said quickly, 'What are you saying about the future of the world?'

'I don't really think it's got much future,' she said, 'at least the way we've got it now.'

'It's an interesting time to be alive,' he said, as though he were still at the party.

'Well, after all,' she said, 'it isn't as though we didn't *know* about it in advance.'

He looked at her for a minute; she was staring absently at the toe of her saddle shoe, moving her foot softly back and forth, following it with her eyes. 'It's really a frightening time when a girl of sixteen has to think of things like that.' In my day, he thought of saying mockingly, girls thought of nothing but cocktails and necking.

'I'm seventeen.' She looked up and smiled at him again. 'There's a terrible difference,' she said.

'In my day,' he said, overemphasizing, 'girls thought of nothing but cocktails and necking.'

'That's partly the trouble,' she answered him seriously. 'If people had been really, honestly scared when you were young we wouldn't be so badly off today.'

His voice had more of an edge than he intended ('When *I* was young!'), and he turned partly away from her as though to indicate the half-interest of an older person being gracious to a child: 'I imagine we thought we were scared. I imagine all kids of sixteen – seventeen – think they're scared. It's part of a stage you go through, like being boy-crazy.'

'I keep figuring how it will be.' She spoke very softly, very clearly, to a point just past him on the wall. 'Somehow I think of the churches as going first, before even the Empire State Building. And then all the big apartment houses by the river, slipping down slowly into the water with the people inside. And the schools, in the middle of Latin class maybe, while we're reading Caesar.' She brought her eyes to his face, looking at him in numb excitement. 'Each time we begin a chapter in Caesar, I wonder if this won't be the one we never finish. Maybe we in our Latin class will be the last people who ever read Caesar.'

'That would be good news,' he said lightly. 'I used to hate Caesar.'

'I suppose when you were young everyone hated Caesar,' she said coolly.

He waited for a minute before he said, 'I think it's a little silly for you to fill your mind with all this morbid trash. Buy yourself a movie magazine and settle down.'

'I'll be able to get all the movie magazines I want,' she said insistently. 'The subways will crash through, you know, and the little magazine stands will all be squashed. You'll be able to pick up all the candy bars you want, and magazines, and lipsticks and artificial flowers from the five-and-ten, and dresses lying in the street from all the big stores. And fur coats.'

'I hope the liquor stores will break wide open,' he said, beginning to feel impatient with her, 'I'd walk in and help myself to a case of brandy and never worry about anything again.'

'The office buildings will be just piles of broken stones,' she said, her wide emphatic eyes still looking at him. 'If only you could know exactly what *minute* it will come.'

'I see,' he said. 'I go with the rest. I see.'

'Things will be different afterward,' she said. 'Everything that makes the world like it is now will be gone. We'll have new rules and new ways of living. Maybe there'll be a law not to live in houses, so then no one can hide from anyone else, you see.'

'Maybe there'll be a law to keep all seventeen-year-old girls in school learning sense,' he said, standing up.

'There won't be any schools,' she said flatly. 'No one will learn anything. To keep from getting back where we are now.'

'Well,' he said, with a little laugh. 'You make it sound very interesting. Sorry I won't be there to see it.' He stopped, his shoulder against the swinging door into the dining-room. He wanted badly to say something adult and scathing, and yet he was afraid of showing her that he had listened to her, that when he was young people had not talked like that. 'If you have any trouble with your Latin,' he said finally, 'I'll be glad to give you a hand.'

She giggled, shocking him. 'I still do my homework every night,' she said.

Back in the living-room, with people moving cheerfully around him, the group by the piano now singing 'Home on the Range,' his hostess deep in earnest conversation with a tall, graceful man in a blue suit, he found the girl's father and said, 'I've just been having a very interesting conversation with your daughter.'

His host's eye moved quickly around the room. 'Eileen? Where is she?'

'In the kitchen. She's doing her Latin.'

' "*Gallia est omnia divisa in partes tres,*" ' his host said without expression. 'I know.'

'A really extraordinary girl.'

His host shook his head ruefully. 'Kids nowadays,' he said.

RYŪNOSUKE AKUTAGAWA *Hell Screen*

KINGSLEY AMIS *Dear Illusion*

SAUL BELLOW *Him With His Foot in His Mouth*

DONALD BARTHELME *Some of Us Had Been Threatening Our
Friend Colby*

SAMUEL BECKETT *The Expelled*

JORGE LUIS BORGES *The Widow Ching – Pirate*

PAUL BOWLES *The Delicate Prey*

ITALO CALVINO *The Queen's Necklace*

ALBERT CAMUS *The Adulterous Woman*

TRUMAN CAPOTE *Children on Their Birthdays*

ANGELA CARTER *Bluebeard*

RAYMOND CHANDLER *Killer in the Rain*

EILEEN CHANG *Red Rose, White Rose*

G. K. CHESTERTON *The Strange Crime of John Boulnois*

JOSEPH CONRAD *Youth*

ROBERT COOVER *Romance of the Thin Man and the
Fat Lady*

ISAK DINESEN *Babette's Feast*

MARGARET DRABBLE *The Gifts of War*

HANS FALLADA *Short Treatise on the Joys of Morphinism*

F. SCOTT FITZGERALD *Babylon Revisited*

IAN FLEMING *The Living Daylights*

E. M. FORSTER *The Machine Stops*

SHIRLEY JACKSON *The Tooth*

HENRY JAMES *The Beast in the Jungle*

M. R. JAMES *Canon Alberic's Scrap-Book*

JAMES JOYCE *Two Gallants*

FRANZ KAFKA *In the Penal Colony*

RUDYARD KIPLING *'They'*

D. H. LAWRENCE *Odour of Chrysanthemums*

PRIMO LEVI *The Magic Paint*

H. P. LOVECRAFT *The Colour Out Of Space*

MALCOLM LOWRY *Lunar Caustic*

CARSON MCCULLERS *Wunderkind*

KATHERINE MANSFIELD *Bliss*

ROBERT MUSIL *Flypaper*

VLADIMIR NABOKOV *Terra Incognita*

R. K. NARAYAN *A Breath of Lucifer*

FRANK O'CONNOR *The Cornet-Player Who Betrayed Ireland*

DOROTHY PARKER *The Sexes*

LUDMILLA PETRUSHEVSKAYA *Through the Wall*

JEAN RHYS *La Grosse Fifi*

SAKI *Filboid Studge, the Story of a Mouse That Helped*

ISAAC BASHEVIS SINGER *The Last Demon*

WILLIAM TREVOR *The Mark-2 Wife*

JOHN UPDIKE *Rich in Russia*

H. G. WELLS *The Door in the Wall*

EUDORA WELTY *Moon Lake*

P. G. WODEHOUSE *The Crime Wave at Blandings*

VIRGINIA WOOLF *The Lady in the Looking-Glass*

STEFAN ZWEIG *Chess*

a little history

Penguin Modern Classics were launched in 1961, and have been shaping the reading habits of generations ever since.

The list began with distinctive grey spines and evocative pictorial covers – a look that, after various incarnations, continues to influence their current design – and with books that are still considered landmark classics today.

Penguin Modern Classics have caused scandal and political change, inspired great films and broken down barriers, whether social, sexual or the boundaries of language itself. They remain the most provocative, groundbreaking, exciting and revolutionary works of the last 100 years (or so).

In 2011, on the fiftieth anniversary of the Modern Classics, we're publishing fifty Mini Modern Classics: the very best short fiction by writers ranging from Beckett to Conrad, Nabokov to Saki, Updike to Wodehouse. Though they don't take long to read, they'll stay with you long after you turn the final page.

MODERN CLASSICS
www.penguinclassics.com